SAM'S Christmas Joy

for Mom and Pop

written by Rebekah Stion
illustrated by Lorraine Arthur

Library of Congress Catalog Card Number 87-91996
© 1988. The STANDARD PUBLISHING Company, Cincinnati, Ohio
Division of STANDEX INTERNATIONAL Corporation. Printed in U.S.A.

"Sam, it's just three days until Christmas," said Dean as he marked another day off on the calendar. And then Dean remembered that this would be Sam's second Christmas with him. He and Sam were special friends.

"I'm ready for bed, Sam. Are you?" asked Dean as he turned back Sam's blanket.

Sam climbed into his bed, and Dean gave him a big hug and a pat on the head.

Then Dean knelt beside his bed to say his prayers. He thought about Christmas. He thought about the suggestion their minister had made that everyone give a gift to someone this Christmas who could not give one back to them. He had called it a Christmas Joy Gift and said that this was a wonderful way to share God's love at Christmas.

Dean began to pray, "Dear God, I love You. I want to do something special this Christmas. I want to give a Christmas Joy Gift. Please help me know what to do. Thank You for loving me. Good-night, God. Good-night, Sam," said Dean.

The next morning at breakfast Dean talked with his mother and dad about the Christmas Joy Gift he wanted to give. They had been thinking about something that the family could do, too.

Dean's mother paused a moment before she spoke.

"Dean," she said, "I know something that we can do. You know Mr. and Mrs. Donaldson who live down the road from us. They are old and cannot go anywhere to buy gifts. We could make gift baskets of fruit, cookies, and cake. Then tomorrow on Christmas Eve you and Sam could take the baskets to them."

A gleam danced in Dean's eyes. He was excited! That was the answer to his prayer. He knew that Mr. and Mrs. Donaldson would be happy, too.

Sam wagged his tail and jumped onto Dean's lap. He could sense something good was happening!

On Christmas Eve, Dean's mother went shopping. She had to purchase the fruit and baskets for the goodies.

Dean and Sam waited eagerly for her return. They met her as soon as she pulled into the driveway. Dean gladly helped carry in the shopping bags. Sam rushed back and forth with Dean.

"Dean and Sam, I've got something to show you!" said Mother excitedly as she unpacked a shopping bag.

She reached into the shopping bag and pulled out a large basket. She handed it to Dean. Then she reached back into the bag and pulled out a very small basket.

"This one is for Sam to give to Mr. and Mrs. Donaldson," said Mother.

"Oh, Mother!" said Dean. "Thank you! I'm happy that Sam can have a part in our Christmas Joy Gift!"

Putting the goodies in the baskets was fun. Dean's mother tied a big red bow around each basket. They were beautiful.

"Mother, can Sam and I take them now?" asked Dean.

His mother knew that he was eager for Mr. and Mrs. Donaldson to see the beautiful baskets.

"Yes, Dean, you and Sam may go now," she said.

Dean placed the small basket around Sam's neck. Sam seemed to understand that he was to carry it. Dean picked up the large basket and called for Sam to follow.

Dean hummed a Christmas carol as they walked down the road toward Mr. and Mrs. Donaldson's house. Sam held his head high so the basket would not slip off his neck. They had only gone a short distance when Dean noticed that Sam's neighborhood dog friends were coming toward them.

"Sam, some of your friends are coming, too!" exclaimed Dean.

Every time that Sam and Dean walked in their neighborhood, Sam's dog friends always joined them. But it was nice to have friends, and Dean knew that Sam enjoyed his friends.

Dean watched Sam as he marched like a soldier, looking straight ahead. His dog friends walked close behind him. Dean was glad that Sam's friends were coming along, too. This would really make Mr. and Mrs. Donaldson know that they were special.

Dean, Sam, and Sam's friends all stopped at the Donaldson's front door. Dean rang the doorbell. Several minutes passed ... then the door opened. There stood Mr. and Mrs. Donaldson with surprised looks on their faces.

"Hello! Mr. and Mrs. Donaldson. We've come to give you a Christmas Joy Gift," said Dean as he handed them his basket.

Mr. and Mrs. Donaldson's eyes filled with tears as they reached for the basket.

Sam walked up and stood in front of them with the little basket still around his neck.

"Sam has one for you, too," said Dean as he slipped it off Sam's neck. "And his friends came along. We all want to wish you a Christmas filled with joy," continued Dean.

Mr. and Mrs. Donaldson looked at the cards attached to the baskets. Both cards read the same "A CHRISTMAS JOY GIFT from our house to your house. Love, Dean and Sam."

The Donaldsons thanked Dean and Sam for the Christmas Joy Gifts. Then they hugged Dean and gave Sam and his dog friends a pat on the head.

As they all said good-bye, there was a special joy in Dean's heart. Giving the gifts to Mr. and Mrs. Donaldson had made him so happy, and he was proud of Sam. Dean stopped and gave Sam a big hug.

"Sam, we must keep the joy of giving in our hearts all year," said Dean as they ran happily toward home.